Santa Claus
and the
Molokai Mules

Written by Jeffrey Garcia
Illustrated by Jamie Meckel

This book was completed because my son Riley taught me to believe in myself and,
for the record, Jamie paints with pixie dust!

Santa Claus and the Molokai Mules

Copyright © 2009 by Jeffrey M. Garcia.

Summary: A boy learns to surf and saves Christmas for Hawaii, receiving a new surfboard from Santa Claus.

ISBN 978-0-9840942-0-2

For information on this book please visit: www.scmmbook.com

First published in the United States in 2010
First Edition
Printed in China

Distributed in USA by Sunbelt Publications
San Diego, California www.sunbeltbooks.com

Kala watched the surfers riding the last few waves as the large orange sun set on the rocky coastline of Molokai.

Kala dreamed of someday gliding across the water, standing up on a real surfboard.

Kala first began riding waves on his tummy with a soft boogie board.

On Molokai, one of the smallest Hawaiian Islands, a young boy or *menehune* must first learn to surf on a boogie board. That's because most of the beaches are too rocky to bodysurf.

Kala couldn't wait to grow up and get his very own surfboard to ride.

From Kala's school, he could see the sleepy town and the island's large lava rock formations that drop off into the great blue Pacific Ocean.

Christmas would be here soon and Kala's neighbors had decorated the town with festive red ribbons and beautiful white plumeria flowers.

The warm and heavy air mixed with the ocean's mist and the sweet scent of the Hawaiian flowers.

Each afternoon when Kala finished school, he met his father to help with the mules.

An expert guide, Kala's father took visitors on tours of the island on the world famous Molokai Mules.

Kala had a favorite mule — one with a beautiful deep brown coat and big wide eyes. He was smaller than the other mules, yet very quick and nimble on the steep trails.

Kala remembered being a very young boy the day the mule was born. Kala helped give the baby mule his first bottle and named him Leap, because he was a great little jumper.

Kala now helped his father train Leap to become one of the pack mules.

When Leap saw Kala, he became so excited that he would kick his hind legs skyward and "Heee-haaa" as loud as he could. Kala would holler back and the two of them made a ruckus loud enough to be heard in the heavens above.

After all of the pack mules settled down for the evening, Kala and his father would take Leap and his father's mule up a narrow and twisting switchback trail. The steep path led to Kimo's Peak, a magnificent lookout named after Kala's grandfather.

On this particular December afternoon, Kala and his father could see that the surf was absolutely perfect at the Molokai Beach Park.

"Whooo-hooo!" shouted Kala's father. "Did you see that wave? It peeled all the way across the bay. Whooo-hooo!"

Kala and his father knew the Hawaiian sun would set by 6:30, which meant if they hurried, they would still have two hours of surfing.

When they got to the beach, Kala's father rubbed a fragrant flower-scented wax on the top of his surfboard for extra grip when riding.

As they paddled out, they watched a skillful rider on a shiny red surfboard. He weaved his way inside the tunneling tube of the wave and flew out the end.

Kala and his father hooted at the top of their lungs. The rider was Kala's brother Johnny, one of the best surfers on Molokai.

After riding a few waves up the point, Kala's father paddled inside to where Kala and the *menehunes* were boogie boarding.

"You are becoming a skillful rider, Kala," said his father. "I think it's time to try my surfboard on some of these beautiful waves."

He slid his board over to Kala and placed his large steady hand on Kala's back, moving him gently into the proper position.

"Relax Kala, and jump to your feet quickly as you catch the next wave. Keep your knees bent to help your balance, then let your body and the surfboard flow with the wave," said his father in a reassuring voice.

Kala paddled hard, jumped to his feet and rode the wave all the way across the bay. Kala felt a glide and speed that he had never felt before. His whole body tingled with excitement.

At the end of the wave, Kala struggled with his father's large, heavy surfboard. Try as he might, he couldn't turn it around and paddle back across the bay. His father's board was simply too big.

When they came home, Kala's mother was proud to hear of Kala's success.

After Kala finished his homework, he asked his mother for red paper so that he could write to Santa Claus for a special Christmas present.

Kala could hardly sleep that night, wondering if Santa would be able to make a new surfboard for him in time for Christmas.

Dear Santa,

I have been a good boy all year. I have helped my father everyday after school with the mules and completed my homework each night, except for a few times.

Please Santa, please bring me a menehune size shiny red surfboard with a gold lightening bolt on the front.

Sincerely,
Kala

On Christmas Eve, Kala got
out of school early and ran eagerly
up the back trail to help his father
with the mules.

"Ah, Kala, it's a good thing you're here," said
his father. "There's an enormous storm coming.
I need you and Johnny to help put the mules in
their barns before the rain arrives."

The trio got the pack mules safely to the
paddock in record time. Then they set out
on their own mules for Kimo's Peak to
gauge how bad the storm would be.

When they reached the peak, they noticed the wind had switched and now blew fiercely from the north.

Huge waves were breaking at twenty-plus feet on the beach. The three surfers watched in silence as they rode the giant swells in their imaginations.

On the ride back home, they heard the deep rumble of thunder from far out at sea.

Their mules grew restless when they reached the barns. Kala gave Leap a special hug and told him that he would be just fine.

For Christmas Eve, Grandpa Kimo, cousins, aunts and uncles all joined Kala's family to sing Christmas carols and enjoy a traditional *'ohana* celebration.

Kala told Grandpa Kimo about his letter to Santa and the *menehune*-size red surfboard he hoped to get in the morning.

Too excited to sleep, Kala heard the TV newsman's shocking story:

"THE FIERCEST STORM OF THE CENTURY IS TEARING ACROSS THE PACIFIC OCEAN, WITH CLOUD COVER SO THICK THAT SANTA CLAUS AND HIS REINDEER CANNOT FIND THE HAWAIIAN ISLANDS. IT LOOKS AS IF HAWAII WILL MISS CHRISTMAS THIS YEAR."

"I know that you must be very disappointed, Kala," said his father. "Maybe we can think of a way to help Santa."

"I've got it Dad! I've got it!" exclaimed Kala. "I'll go up to Kimo's Peak and hide. You bring Leap up behind me. I'll surprise him and he'll make so much noise that Santa's reindeer are sure to hear him."

"Outstanding Kala!" said his father. "That's an excellent idea, my son."

"Can you make it alone Kala?" asked his father. "It's so dark and the trail will be very slippery."

"Dad, we must save Christmas for Hawaii," said Kala. "I know I can do it!"

"I know you can too," replied his father. "You've been up the trail a hundred times and I'll be just behind you with Leap if you need help."

At first Kala felt frightened, but thinking of all the sad Hawaiian children on Christmas morning gave him courage and strength.

As he went higher, the storm became more and more ferocious. But onward he pushed through the storm of the century.

He did it! Kala reached Kimo's Peak before his father and Leap.

He hid behind a lava rock and waited patiently for them to arrive.

Just as they reached the peak, Kala sprang up screaming,
"Leap, Leap!"

Leap reared up in excitement, jumping up and down and letting
out a "Heee-haaa! Heee-haaa! Heee-haaa!" that could be heard
from as far away as the heavens above.

All of a sudden, bells jingled as a bright flash appeared in the sky.

Santa's sleigh swooped down as the reindeer let out a "Heee-haaa" at Leap. Leap heee-haaa'ed back as he jumped up in excitement.

"*Mele Kalikimaka!* Merry Christmas, Kala!" cheered Santa as he pulled up on the reins.

Kala turned to his father, who smiled from ear to ear.

"You did it Kala!" exclaimed his father. "You saved Christmas for all of Hawaii!"

In the morning, an excited Kala ran out to the living room, where he immediately spied the shiniest red surfboard he had ever seen. He had never felt happier in his entire life.

As he looked into the brilliant gold lightning bolt, Santa's face slowly appeared and gave Kala a long, steady wink before the face disappeared back into the board. Kala felt a warm glow over his entire body.

Kala turned the surfboard over to feel the board's smooth bottom. There he found a special message: *"Thank you Kala & always surf with joy, Santa."*

Mahalo plenty to:

My wife Julie for her kind, loving and supportive soul.

Oliver, my son, for his infectious laugh and making the world smile.

Martha Lambert for her storyline suggestions and the most encouraging energy on earth.

Bruce Jenkins for acknowledging my writing.

Katy Kissel for the strength of her comments through reserve and integrity.

Maria Zegallo and her literary class in England for their critical feedback.

Lisa Cohen, the greatest teacher on earth, and her third grade class for their supportive letters.

Charlotte Brown for introducing me to Mark Michelon, who introduced me to Jamie Meckel.

Patricia Buckley for her cool demeanor and professional children's book editing.

Mary Gallagher for her fine-line editorial assistance.

Codi Watt for her pre-press expertise and file management.

Jamie would like to acknowledge her wonderful parents and Dwight for all of their love and support.